Can You See Me Now?

Minister
Bertram "Be'Jay" Major

ENTEGRITY
CHOICE PUBLISHING

Entegrity Choice Publishing
PO Box 453
Powder Springs, GA 30127
info@entegritypublishing.com
www.entegritypublishing.com
770.727.6517

Printed in the United States of America

Library of Congress Cataloging-in-Publication Data
ISBN: 978-1-7351739-7-9
Library of Congress Control Number: 2020919140

Dedication

Firstly, all honor and glory belongs to God! He has truly seen me through this process. This particular book was not planned, it was given to me after a Facebook live video I did in April 2020.

The journey was rough and I was unsure at how I was going to get this done. God saw me through and He sent several people my way that encouraged me during this writing journey of this book, "Can You See Me Now?"

To my staff at BEJM Ministries:

Yasmine: For always encouraging me and not being afraid to share your thoughts. You have really played an important part in this journey and I appreciate all that you do!

Cedric: I always learn a lot from you. You always inspire me to think outside of the box when it comes to ministry. This book has me truly thinking AND stepping outside of the box and I'm forever grateful for all that you do!

There is one more staff member who I will mention at the end of this dedication. I have a lot to say about her.

Thank you Mom, Dad, and grandmother, MaMa, for your continuous support. You all have truly been a HUGE help over the years! God really blessed me by sending me to be with y'all. I'm the blessed one because you all are amazing people who have shown me love and support. Thank you and I love you all.

Of course, I have to give a shout out to my Pastor Chavous Boyd and the Mt. Zion Missionary Baptist Church of Augusta, Georgia. You showed me so much support when I published my first book. You have never stopped encouraging me—you encouraged me to keep writing. To be honest, I have been so overwhelmed with thanks and fire to keep writing since then. I love you all!

To my Young Adult Small Group class—well, let me rephrase that—my Young Adult Small Group FAMILY: Jamelda, Kayla, Tanetra, Annisha, Asia, and one more person who I will talk about at the end of this dedication.

I'm about to be so real with the words I am about to say. I was so close to giving up teaching the young adult class. Teaching was something

God led me to do and when I was finally allowed to do the class, I was excited and nervous. As time went on, I felt so discouraged because of the lack of attendance. But God kept telling me to hold on. There were times I felt as if I was letting God down. I felt that what I was doing was not helping other young adults come to Christ.

I started to ease up on myself a lot. I asked God to show me what to do. Once COVID-19 started, we went from doing everything at church once a week to going virtual. Our class has become more of a small group setting than Bible study. We grew in number, and started to reach other people in other places. You will never know how much you mean to me by just showing up and allowing me to teach and help you. In the process, you have taught and helped me as well. Thank you so much for your continuous support during this journey! In my first book, I talked about how I asked God to surround me with young people ON FIRE for Christ. Well, since then, He has done just that!

To my friends I have connected with since the release of my first book through Facebook, Instagram, and those I've met in person: GJ, Shanna, Melondy, Lisa, Tahlea, Armani, Bria, Katuscia, Alexandra, Kalyse, John (Mighty Sanchez), Ti'geria,

Christina, Tatyana, and Dafney —you have all truly been a huge support over the past few years! You are truly an answered prayer. I love each and every single one of you.

And finally, to that special someone I saved for the end: my assistant in my ministry and part of my Young Adult Small Group. Most importantly, as of this writing, she is my fiancé! By the time I finish my next book, that will be changed. To my beautiful fiancé, Kaylin. You came into my life months after my first book was published. It's amazing how we have mutual connections and went to the same schools at times but did not officially meet until we were adults. You have been a breath of fresh air, my backbone, my best friend, my headache (sometimes), my travel partner—I can go on and on.

Most importantly, you are a God-fearing woman with vision. You are the woman God sent to me! You are the woman who will become my wife in the very near future. One day, you are going to be the mother of my kids. I can see myself doing a lot with you in life. We have had some great times together! I know for a fact, that the best is truly still yet to come. I love you, My Queen. You stayed on me so much when it came to writing this book. You encouraged me to take an entire month off from ministry just to rest, reconnect with God, and to finish a lot of things I needed to get done—one of which was this book. I was able to finish this book during that one-month break. The future is looking so bright. I love you. I'm so blessed to have you in my life. You are truly my Helpmeet (That's the King James Version).

To all of you reading this, this book is dedicated to you as well. Thank you for not just purchasing this book but taking the time to read it. My prayer is that you truly receive something out of this book that helps you in your walk with Christ.

May God Bless and Keep You All.

Contents

Introduction

"Now Thomas, called the Twin, one of the twelve, was not with them when Jesus came. The other disciples therefore said to him, "We have seen the Lord." So he said to them, "Unless I see in His hands the print of the nails, and put my finger into the print of the nails, and put my hand into His side, I will not believe." And after eight days His disciples were again inside, and Thomas with them. Jesus came, the doors being shut, and stood in the midst, and said, "Peace to you!" Then He said to Thomas, "Reach your finger here, and look at My hands; and reach your hand here, and put it into My side. Do not be unbelieving, but believing." And Thomas answered and said to Him, "My Lord and my God!" Jesus said to him, "Thomas, because you have seen Me, you have believed. Blessed are those who have not seen and yet have believed." John 20:24-29 (NKJV)

On Thursday, April 16, 2020, I delivered a message on Facebook Live titled, "Can you see me now?" That message was based on this very scripture. The following morning, the Lord spoke to me and I wrote down everything He told me and turned it into a spoken-word piece. That Sunday, I shared it on social media. Here is what the Lord spoke on the morning after I delivered the message:

> *Why are you mad?*
> *You got what you wanted.*
> *You said you wanted more time.*
> *Time to rest.*
> *Time to plan.*
> *Time to get yourself together.*
> *Time to spend with your family.*
> *You even wanted more time to spend with me.*
> *But you're still mad?*
> *You still not satisfied?*
> *I gave you just what you asked for.*
> *But it's not enough?*
>
> *Okay, the way I gave you all this time may not have been the way you wanted but I did what I thought was best.*

*When you said you wanted more time, I took
that seriously.*
I heard your cry and your plea.
*When COVID-19 started, I saw a chance not
just to protect you, but a chance to spend time
with you by answering your prayer.*

So, I shut down the schools.
I shut down the workplaces.
I shut down your hangouts.
I shut down the barbershops and beauty salons.
I even shut down the church buildings.

I had to break routines, get rid of distractions.
*Even with shutting down the beauty salons and
barbershops, I had to do that because I want you
to focus more on your inside instead of your
outside.*
*I even shut down the church buildings because
I wanted you to learn more about how to BE the
church instead of just going to church.*

I did not do this to be mean.
I'm just answering your prayer.
*Out of all the reasons, you stated about
wanting more time, there was only one reason*

that stood out the most.

When you said, "Lord I need more time to spend with you," I knew I had to make that happen.

See, I've got COVID-19 already handled; I will get you through this. Leave that in my hands. But I have used this chance to answer your prayer about more time.

Can you see me now?
Can you see who I am now?
I gave you just what you wanted and then some.

Do you believe me?
Do you trust me?
I have performed miracle after miracle not just to be doing it but I did it so that you could see who I am.

I remained faithful to you through all the sins and excuses.
All I want from you is a relationship.
You don't have to just hear about me, come and get to know me.
I did my part.
I ask again, "Can you see me now?"

*If you don't, there is going to be a time when
you do see me.
I'm going to get word from my Father to go get
every born-again believer: Those in the grave
and alive.
I'm going to bring them all up to Heaven with
me.
If you can't see me now,
You and so many others will see me then.*

*I don't want you to be left behind.
Do you remember what I said in Matthew
11:28-30?
I got you, My Child!
But do you want me?*

*When you asked for more time, were you just
making another excuse?
I see the real you and I still love you!
I still want a relationship with you, but do you
want one with me?
Can you see me now?*

*People have come and gone in your life.
I've never left your side.
So many people have been fake to you but I've
always been real.*

*I'm waiting on you but I urge you not to hold
off much longer.*

*I can do more than what a vaccine can do.
My blood can clean and disinfect better than
hand sanitizer and soap.
I can supply more needs than a stimulus check
can.
I'm more powerful than a pandemic.
I AM That I AM!
Me and My Father are one!*

*I did what I did because I want you to get to
know me and trust me.
Do you have time now?
Can you see me now?*

Since then, this title, "Can you see me now?"
has been replaying in my head. I'm writing this
book in the mist of the COVID-19 pandemic. My
heart bleeds for those who wanted more time to
spend with God but choose to flat out ignore Him.
Change is not an event; it is a process. That is a
true fact; however, it's often used as an excuse.
Even though it's a process, you are going to have
to start that process at some point. When is your
starting point?

This pandemic has affected us all in some shape, form, or fashion. Thomas refused to believe Jesus had risen. He said the only way he would believe is if he saw the print of the nails in His hands, put his finger into the print of the nails, and put his hand into His side. Eight days after he said this, Jesus appeared to His disciples (including Thomas). Jesus greeted them and, afterwards, told Thomas to put his finger into the print of the nails in His hand. Jesus also told Thomas to get his hand and put it in His side. After that Jesus said, "Do not be unbelieving, but believing."All Thomas could say was, "My Lord and My God!" In John 20:29, Jesus said,*"Thomas, because you have seen me, you have believed. Blessed are those who have not seen and yet have believed."*

It's amazing that Jesus did all that just for one person to really see Him for who He is. Now, a lot of people to this day say that, I will not believe Jesus Christ is the Son of God unless He does this or that, or if those who believe can prove this or prove that. Thomas was blessed enough to be granted exactly what he wanted in the way he wanted.

However, Jesus may not show Himself in the way you want or like He did for Thomas. You have to be open and willing to see Jesus for who He is in the way He shows you. In this book, God will use me to minister to all of you about how important it is to get to know Jesus. The question the Lord Jesus is asking is, "Can You See Me Now?" He granted Thomas's request and Thomas saw Him for who He truly was all along.

I'm going to break down this spoken word and clearly explain everything that the Lord wants me to share. You may still have a lot of questions you want answered. All I can say is buckle up and join me on this journey of trying to see and getting to know who Jesus Christ is. I guarantee this one thing, if you truly open your heart and allow the Holy Spirit to move through you while reading this, your life will definitely never be the same again.

Let us pray.

Father God,

As we take this journey, I pray that everyone who is about to read this book is touched, encouraged, convicted, and changed. Lord, we decrease so that you may increase. Enlarge our territory and keep your hands upon us so no evil will harm us. Lord, I pray that after everyone reaches the end of this book, they will be able to answer the question, "Can you see me now?" with a strong YES! Let Your will be done through the story that is about to be told. I say this prayer in the mighty name of Jesus Christ.

Amen

1
Be Careful What You Ask For You Just Might Get It

Why are you mad?
You got what you wanted.
You said you wanted more time.
Time to rest.
Time to plan.
Time to get yourself together.
Time to spend with your family.

You even wanted more time to spend with me.
But you're still mad?
You're still not satisfied?
I gave you just what you asked for.
But it's not enough?

Okay, the way I gave you all this time may not have been the way you wanted, but I did what I thought was best.
When you said you wanted more time, I took that seriously.
I heard your cry and your plea.
When COVID-19 started, I saw a chance not just to protect you, but a chance to spend time with you by answering your prayer.

God has His way of answering prayer, he's always does what's best.

"For My thoughts are not your thoughts, Nor are your ways My ways," says the Lord. "For as the heavens are higher than the earth, So are My ways higher than your ways, And My thoughts than your thoughts." Isaiah 55:8-9 (NKJV)

A lot of people forget that God is God and that it's not our job to do His job. The way He works is not the way we work. I asked someone a question a while back. I asked, "If God showed exactly how He does things, would you be able to comprehend it all?"

His thoughts, ways, timing, and reasoning has a purpose. In the midst of everything that happens in the world, God will find a way to use it for His glory. I'm not saying He caused COVID-19, hate, racism, or injustice. What I am saying is that in the midst of pain, confusion, sickness, distress, or death, GOD IS THERE!

"God is our refuge and strength, A very present help in trouble." Psalm 46:1 (KJV)

During this pandemic, so many people are seeking answers and guidance from everything and everyone but God. God has used this time to answer probably one of the most requested prayers, "Lord, give me more time." He has given each of us more time in some shape, form, or fashion. The sad truth is, if prayers are not answered the way some people want, they won't receive what God has done. One thing I strongly believe is that God's word is final! You can speak into existence everything you want but if it's not a part of God's will, it won't happen. Jeremiah 29:11 is one of the most quoted scriptures. I must say, a lot of people quote it but don't really understand it. It sounds great but there's a story behind every verse. You must clearly read it and understand it. Now, I highly recommend you read everything that leads up to Jeremiah 29:11. But in the interest of time, I want to focus on just this one verse to make a point. When we look at the verse itself, we come to one huge conclusion. Let's take a look:

> ***"For I know the thoughts that I think toward you, says the LORD, thoughts of peace and not of evil, to give you a future and a hope."***
> ***Jeremiah 29:11 (KJV)***

God knows the plans!
God knows!
Yes, He said plans to prosper and not harm and, yes, plans to give hope and a future. Now, I challenge you to go and read everything that leads up to this verse. But the huge conclusion we

can come to is that God knows! Does that mean everything will work out the way we want? Not at all!

I just thank God that it's going to work out. Don't be so caught up with how good something sounds and forget to understand the meaning. I think we forget that when things don't work out our way, it is not really a bad thing. But as long as it works out God's way, that's all that matters. When you are able to look at everything in your life and say,"It's all good because it's all God," you realize the ultimate fact: God's Way is always the right way!

I challenge you all to make time for God and don't put anything or anyone in His place. I recently posted,*"The reason you can't see God or believe He exists is because you have other things and other people in His place."*

Always be mindful of what you ask God; you just might get it. I'm going to end this chapter with two questions:

"Have you made room for God?"

"Are you prepared to receive what you have prayed to God about?"

Ask yourself these questions and be sure to answer them to yourself.

2

Being Shut Down Doesn't Mean You Are Shut Out

> *So, I shut down the schools.*
> *I shut down the workplaces.*
> *I shut down your hangouts.*
> *I shut down the barbershops and beauty salons.*
> *I even shut down the church buildings.*
>
> *I had to break routines, get rid of distractions.*
> *Even with shutting down the beauty salons and*
> *barbershops, I had to do that because I want you*
> *to focus more on your inside instead of your*
> *outside.*
> *I even shut down the church buildings because*
> *I wanted you to learn more about how to BE the*
> *church instead of just going to church.*
>
> *I'm not do this to be mean.*
> *I'm just answering your prayer.*

I strongly believe so many people are missing out on a huge life-changing opportunity. I'm not just talking about life on the earthly side, I'm talking about life eternal. So many forget that life on this side is temporary. Yes, we have responsibilities we must fulfill and can't avoid a lot that's happening in the world. However, none of us should be making permanent plans for a temporary situation. I constantly hear the cliché,

"Don't be so heavenly bound that you are no earthly good." I totally agree! For example, a lot of people are saying that they are not going to wear a mask because God will protect them. God is a protector, but He gives us common sense and knowledge! In Matthew 4:7, when Satan tried to get Jesus to cave in and defy the Father's will, Jesus replied, *"It is also written: "Do not put the Lord your God to the test."*

In other words, don't tempt God! We can have faith in God and wear a mask. In other words, you can still love and trust God and use common sense. This cliché is important and true but we must keep in mind, *"Don't be so earthly planted that you are not heavenly rooted."*

Pay attention to everything that's going on. God has gone to extreme measures to get everybody's attention. He shut down everything and got rid of so many distractions, so people can see Him. Too many people get too caught up in the routines and habits sometimes that they forget about God. So many people say they love and know the Lord but don't know anything about Him. Something a lot of people are guilty of is lip service. They say one thing but do something else. God's love is precious but very tough at the same time.

When everything was being shut down, I think a lot of people were looking at things through their natural eye instead of their spiritual eye. It's like people are looking at how much they have lost instead of realizing what they are gaining.

I strongly believe we are in the last days and we are close to the return of our Lord and Savior, Jesus Christ. God is truly not playing games at all! He's getting ready to sound the alarm and tell His Son, Jesus Christ, to go get My Children. With that being said, God has gone to extreme measures to get us to get serious. He has given His Son and it's time to make an important decision. Just because God shut down a lot of places and distractions doesn't mean WE are shut OUT.

3
There's Reasoning Behind Everything

Out of all the reasons, you stated about wanting more time, there was only one reason that stood out the most.
When you said, "Lord I need more time to spend with you," I knew I had to make that happen.

See, I've got COVID-19 already handled; I will get you through this. Leave that in my hands. But I have used this chance to answer your prayer about more time.

Can you see me now?
Can you see who I am now?

I gave you just what you wanted and then some.
Do you believe me?
Do you trust me?
I have performed miracle after miracle not just to be doing it, but I did it so that you could see who I am.

I remained faithful to you through all the sins and excuses.
All I want from you is a relationship.
You don't have to just hear about me, come and get to know me.

I did my part.
I ask again, "Can you see me now?"

One thing I have come to realize over the past several years is that the Lord truly does answer prayer. However, He doesn't always answer them the way we want. For example, you may ask Him for a "boo" who is genuine, loving, and looks a certain way. Then, when He answers your prayer, the person He sends you is genuine, loving, but the looks may not be what you prayed for. God has His reasoning behind everything He does. A lot of people would rejoice in the fact that their prayer has been answered. But sadly, for some, if an answered prayer doesn't line up to everything they want, they reject it and some even rebel against God. Just imagine the missed opportunities, relationships, elevations, new house, or new cars so many have missed out on all because the answer didn't meet every requirement on their list. One of the big problems I see in today's world is that God has been so good to the point that some people have become spoiled children.

I'm so glad that God know us and does what He knows best for us. You cannot say I love and trust God but then get mad because He doesn't do things 100% the way you want Him to do them. This pandemic is being used by the Lord to show the importance of getting the attention of all people, saved and unsaved. It's time for everyone to stop leaning on their own understanding and to completely lean on God.

When it comes to a spoiled person, one thing that needs to happen is that they need to get over themselves and grow up. God has given this world a gift, His Son, Jesus Christ. Spiritual immaturity has so many heading to Hell—most don't even realize it. God's reasoning is final! Either you can accept it or not.

Keep this in mind. God is faithful and will never leave you high and dry. He will never let you down and all He wants is a relationship with those who truly want to get to know Him.

"For God so loved the world, that He gave His only begotten Son, that whosoever believeth in Him should not perish, but have everlasting life." John 3:16 (KJV)

Through Jesus Christ, you not only have everything you need but you gain an "Assurance Policy." It's great to know you can have a real and honest relationship with God through His Son, Jesus Christ. You don't have to wait to get to Heaven for that, you can have that right now. What a joyous and wonderful day it will be when we get to Heaven! Just imagine having a relationship with Jesus during your time here on Earth. Then when your life is over on this side, you get to be with Him forever! So basically, when it comes to the Lord's blessing, our response should be, "Any way you bless me Lord, I'll be satisfied."

Don't be blinded by not having your way; just rejoice in the fact that God is having His way. I want you to say this to yourself but say it with conviction:

"God will never fail me."

"God knows what's best for me."

Without the Lord, not only are we nothing, our life will be even more in a mess than it already is. It would be like driving a car in the dark with no headlights. Let's look at Proverbs 3:5-6 not just as a popular verse but let's truly, wholeheartedly apply this to our lives and let it marinate in our souls:

"Trust in the Lord with all your heart, And lean not on your own understanding; In all your ways acknowledge Him, And He shall direct your paths." Proverbs 3:5-6 (NKJV)

4

You Will See Me, Sooner or Later

> *If you don't, there is going to be a time when*
> *you do see me.*
> *I'm going to get word from my Father to go get*
> *every born-again believer, Those in the grave*
> *and alive.*
> *I'm going to bring them all up to Heaven with*
> *me.*
> *If you can't see me now.*
> *You and so many others will see me then.*
>
> *I don't want you to be left behind.*
> *Do you remember what I said in*
> *Matthew 11:28-30?*
> *I got you my child!*
> *But do you want me?*

Whether you want to believe it or not, Jesus is coming back. You know when it comes to the Bible, so many people pick and choose what they want to believe and apply to their life. In other words, some people want full-time benefits from God but are only giving Him part-time attention. Having a relationship with Jesus sounds so good until that relationship starts to change you and your life. I will discuss this further in Chapter 8.

Growing up, I felt differently and wanted the attention and approval of my peers. It's like

I would have done anything for that. I wanted them to accept me for me but I wasn't being me. I was trying to be someone I wasn't. You have to be careful with people because you will be amazed at how some of them will look good on the outside but are evil and nasty on the inside. The great thing about having Jesus in your life, not only you will have Him as your friend and Savior—but He's real, trustworthy, and will never let you down!

Don't take it lightly, Jesus is coming back! He doesn't want you to be one of those people who avoids the seriousness of being ready for Him and ends up being left behind because of it. As Christians, we must not only warn the lost but we must also hold each other accountable. As I previously said, I strongly believe God has not caused this pandemic. But he's USING this pandemic as a wake-up call for us all. It's up to each individual whether to believe or not believe, but now is truly decision-making time.

What we are currently facing in today's world is nothing compared to The Great Tribulation. A lot of people are trying to state their reasons for not wearing a mask. One of the reasons is because of the Mark of The Beast. Let me break this down. There are some similarities when it comes to wearing a mask and the Mark of the Beast. Some businesses are requiring customers to wear a mask to enter. The Mark of the Beast will be the same way but extremely worse. Taking that mark will automatically make you property of Satan and YOU WILL NOT GO TO HEAVEN! That's just a small snippet of how it will be in The Great Tribulation. However, The Great Tribulation will not happen until after the Rapture of the Church.

Currently we are in the COVID-19 pandemic, not The Great Tribulation! Even though there are similarities, we know the importance of wearing a mask. It's more to protect others than ourselves. As Christians, not only should we love one another but we need to show it. That's what being a Christian is all about! You cannot, and I repeat, CANNOT call yourself a Christian and not show love. Wearing a mask is not about your rights being taking away or the Mark of the Beast. We are not in The Great Tribulation. Calm down and relax. Wearing a mask will protect others (putting love into action) and decrease the spread of COVID-19. Although there are similarities, I do believe God is using those similarities to get us to see that now is the time to get serious about our soul salvation and to put our focus in spreading the Gospel of Jesus Christ.

A lot has happened during this pandemic

and it still is happening. But until that trumpet sounds, we have a mission to fulfill! For those who have not made the decision to accept Jesus Christ, there will come a day when you will realize and declare that He is Lord and Savior! The Rapture of the Church should not be a scary event to talk about for any believer. Being caught up in the air and seeing Jesus in all of His Glory is something you should look forward to.

The reason I talk about The Great Tribulation and the Mark of the Beast, is not to scare anyone into getting saved. It is to help those who have not said *yes* to Jesus. It is said to be living in Hell on Earth and then dying and going to Hell; it's so not worth it. Jesus did not die for you to stay lost, confused, or in bondage. Accept Jesus now and don't put it on hold until later. Later not only isn't promised, but later could have you wishing you would have said *yes* to Jesus when you first had the opportunity. Go to Jesus now, not later!

Trust and believe that you will see Jesus for who He is one day whether you want to accept Him or not. Awake and see how good your life can be through Jesus Christ. Don't take my word for it, do your own research and find out about this man named Jesus.

5
God Still Loves You

> *When you asked for more time, were you just*
> *making another excuse?*
> *I see the real you and I still love you!*
> *I still want a relationship with you, but do you*
> *want one with me?*
>
> *Can you see me now?*
> *People have come and gone in your life.*
> *I've never left your side.*
> *So many people have been fake to you but I've*
> *always been real.*

God sent His only begotten Son not just for me but for each and every one of you who are reading this, for your family, friends, coworkers, classmates, strangers you see every day, and even the people you see on TV. God sent His Son for everybody! It's up to each individual to accept this gift named Jesus Christ. When you really think about it, we don't even deserve the love He gives us. Because of His unfailing love, we are still here. Waking up every day is another chance from Him. I want each and every one of you to stop and look at your life. I don't want you to look at anyone else's life; look at yours.

Some of you are a walking miracle. Some of you should be locked up. Some of you have been in situations that should have screwed up your life forever. Some of you have actually said, "I dodged a bullet" or "I'm so lucky" or "That was a close one." Some of you have said that but deep down in your heart, you felt that there was more to the story. You have felt not only that you are here for a purpose but you feel that there is something missing in your life.

Let me tell you this, my dear friends. You are a living testimony. God not only has you here because He loves you, He has you here because there is something about you that the world needs to see. Your life is not just a blessing to you, it can be a blessing to others. I don't care what wrong you have done, *God still loves you!* Why not serve Him? He has sent Jesus to save us. The punishment we all deserve has been paid through the blood of Jesus Christ. Some of you think that you are a lost cause because of the sins you have committed. Some of you are saying, "I have rejected the Lord purposely over the years, there's no way He will accept me."

Well guess what?

"If we confess our sins, He is faithful and just to forgive us our sins, and to cleanse us from all unrighteousness. Confess - admit or state that one has committed a crime or is at fault in some way." 1 John 1:9 (KJV)

Confess everything to the Lord and I guarantee you He will forgive you! You must confess everything to Him no matter how bad it is. When you allow the Lord to move in your life, He can cleanse you and make you new. Whatever you tell the Lord, you don't have to worry about it popping up on social media or in a text message. Everything is between you and Him.

I strongly believe we can all testify to the fact that we have had people come and go in our lives. Those same people used to say,"I'm never going anywhere." But now, they are nowhere to be found. Not all people are like that but what I am saying is at the end of the day, the only person you can truly count on 1000% is the Lord!

I think a huge reason some people are not seeing Jesus is because they are too busy giving permanent attention to temporary people. You can't expect to get a promotion without doing the work. You cannot pass a test in school if you don't study. You won't be able to see Jesus with your attention of people, habits, etc. Let me make this clear. I want to rephrase something I said earlier. I said that God sent His only begotten Son to die for us. Let me say it like this, "God sent His Child into this world to die for us." Think about it—HIS CHILD!

I know for a fact that if you ask a parent if they would give their child as a sacrifice for this world, they would say no. I know some of you are not parents (myself included), but think of it like this. Parents sadly lose their children, which hurts. But just imagine a parent giving their child as a sacrifice for you and this whole entire world. Imagine turning on the TV and on the news is a man saying that in order to save the World from sin and give everyone a chance to have eternal life, he's giving his only child. God's love is so real and powerful! God did it! He gave His only begotten Son! That's love right there! Pure love!

You don't have to stay lost; you are not a lost cause! You are a masterpiece. Through Jesus Christ, you are so much more as well. Do not play hot potatoes with your soul, take notice of God's Mercy! He loves you, that's a fact!

Love is an action that not everybody shows but God has and still is currently showing. Morning by morning, brand new mercies are one of the greatest blessings we can all testify to! You are special, loved, and appreciated!

6

The True Remedy

*I'm waiting on you but I urge you not to hold
off much longer.
I can do more than what a vaccine can do.
My blood can clean and disinfect better than
hand sanitizer and soap.
I can supply more needs than a stimulus check
can.*

*I'm more powerful than a pandemic.
I Am That I AM!
Me and My Father are one!
I did what I did because I want you to get to
know me and trust me.*

*Do you have time now?
"Can you see me now?"*

The remedy to the issues and problems of life is Jesus Christ! During the COVID-19 pandemic, one thing that has disturbed me is how some people are putting more trust and faith in doctors, hand sanitizer, masks, and even money. I commend every doctor and essential worker because they have been working so very hard. I understand and agree with the importance of practicing good hygiene and practicing social distancing. Even with finances, it's so important to make sure everything is straight financially. But none of that is the true remedy.

The blood of Jesus Christ is the true remedy to everything. Not just during the pandemic, but even after the Pandemic, the blood of Jesus is the cure. We put so much effort into doing what the doctor says, practicing good hygiene, practicing social distancing, making sure we are being responsible financially; we need to put that same effort (even more effort) into pleading the blood of Jesus Christ! We always need to read the Word of God, always stay in constant prayer, and always keep our eyes on Jesus. At the end of the day, remember who died for you. Your horoscope is not the answer. Your crystals and burning sage are not the way to peace. Some celebrities may say things that sound and feel good but that doesn't make them Godly. Jesus is the remedy! Jesus is the answer; Jesus is your peace; not only is Jesus Godly, He is God! If you don't see any nail marks in someone's hands or nail marks in someone's feet, don't give them the attention you need to be giving Jesus.

It's amazing how the Lord has used a terrible time in the World to show that not only can we trust Him to handle the pandemic but we can trust Him to handle EVERYTHING. All of us need medicine in this Christian walk. Jesus is our physician; go to Him and tell Him the problem. He will give what you need. Some of you have been trying to truly find out more about Jesus.

We hear a lot and see a lot, but we must want to have our own experience with Him. You don't have to search any further. Instead of doing the same old routine, remove some things and replace them with praise and worship, prayer, Bible study, or even doing ministry (volunteer work, spreading the Gospel on the streets, etc.).

Go on a hike or take a trip to relax and communicate with Him. Jesus is the only one that can change you but you have a responsibility, too. Don't ask Him to change you if you are not going to embrace it. Change may not feel good at first and it may not be what you want but it's worth it. You must deny yourself (desires and feelings). Take up your cross. In life, there are times that you must go with the flow and deal with it. Jesus will be by your side every step of the way. Follow Him. The hand of the Lord is knocking at the door of your heart, will you let Him in? Jesus is waiting for each and every one of you. Are you going to let Him in?

7

Drastic Times Calls for Drastic Measures

Drastic is defined as:
Likely to have a strong or far-reaching effect;
radical and extreme.

In life, when something is done out of the ordinary, some people tend to act out differently. Some react in frustration, anger or violence. Some become depressed, confused, reluctant, etc. When COVID-19 started to really get serious, I could tell we were in for an unprecedented journey. A virus that first became endemic and then pandemic. We started to see so many places forced to shut down, including church buildings. Right away, that was a huge wake-up call for me. I also strongly believe that was a huge wake-up call for a lot of people.

When I started to see the church buildings closing their doors due to the pandemic, I knew it was God. I didn't know exactly what the purpose was right at that moment, but I knew it was Him. Now some of you may be saying, "Why would the Lord shut down The Church?"

If you asked that, let me make a correction, The Church did not get shut down, the church buildings did. The Church is the people of God who have been born again by accepting Jesus Christ as Lord and Savior. The church buildings are the meeting places (a spiritual gas station) for the people of God who have been born again. When the Lord spoke to me the morning following my Facebook Live session, He said, "I shut down the church buildings because I wanted you to learn more about how to BE the church instead of just going to the church."

I truly felt His power become stronger at that point. So many people love to get their outfits together, brag about being proud to be Baptist, Church of God in Christ, Pentecostal, etc. Some people love going on social media to talk about how they can't wait to get their shout on, or can't wait to hear their Pastor throw down. So many people get caught up in going to church and not focused at all on BEING the church. It's like going to church had become a trend. When I step into the church building, I am more ready to get the Word of God instead of worrying about my outfit, somebody else's outfit, what songs the choir are going to sing, or how high the preacher is going to hoop. I go to the building to get refilled so I can get more equipped not only for myself but to also tell the world more about Jesus Christ. You cannot call yourself a Christian without spreading the Gospel. A lot of people holding positions in the Church think that their position is their relationship with God. That's a very troubling mindset; it's a mindset so many have.

"Not everyone who says to Me, Lord, Lord, shall enter the kingdom of heaven, but he who does the will of My Father in heaven. Many will say to Me in that day, Lord, Lord, have we not prophesied in Your name, cast out demons in Your name, and done many wonders in Your name? And then I will declare to them, I never knew you; depart from Me, you who practice lawlessness!" Matthew 7:21-23 (NKJV)

What you do in The Church and what you claim to be in Christ doesn't mean a thing at all if you have not accepted Jesus Christ as Lord and Savior. Also, it doesn't mean a thing if you are not following Him daily and doing your best to be an example for Him. You can't say you are for Christ but constantly throwing shade and being petty. You can't say you are for Christ but are being toxic and gossiping about others. You can't say you are for Christ but use your social media accounts as a platform to spread hate, ungodliness, and negativity instead of using them as a platform to make a difference and to bring more understanding to who Jesus is and why it's important to have a relationship with Him.

If I was to bring this up on social media or in a conversation, some people may respond by saying, "Stop being so uptight." None of us are perfect; stop judging. Excuses will never get you anywhere in life. In order to truly experience Jesus Christ and to have a committed relationship with Him, changes must take place. Jesus Christ is the only one who can change your heart, mind, and soul, but we all have a responsibility. Drastic times calls for drastic measures!

Changing your habits and the people you hang out with that are not sharpening you, and eliminating everything that's a danger to your connection with Jesus Christ may be drastic but it's worth it!

8

Stop With The Excuses

Excuse is defined as:
An attempt to lessen the blame attaching to (a
fault or offense); seek to defend or justify.

"Now when one of those who sat at the table
with Him heard these things, he said to Him,
"Blessed is he who shall eat bread in the
kingdom of God!" Then He said to him, "A
certain man gave a great supper and invited
many, and sent his servant at supper time to say
to those who were invited, Come, for all things
are now ready. But they all with one accord
began to make excuses. The first said to him, I
have bought a piece of ground, and I must go
and see it. I ask you to have me excused. And
another said, I have bought five yoke of oxen,
and I am going to test them. I ask you to have
me excused. Still another said, I have married
a wife, and therefore I cannot come. So that
servant came and reported these things to his
master. Then the master of the house, being
angry, said to his servant, Go out quickly into
the streets and lanes of the city, and bring in here
the poor and the maimed and the lame and the
blind. And the servant said, Master, it is done
as you commanded, and still there is room. Then
the master said to the servant, Go out into the

highways and hedges, and compel them to come in, that my house may be filled. For I say to you that none of those men who were invited shall taste my supper." Luke 14:15-24 (NKJV)

In January 2020 at my first ministry event for the year, me and a few friends did a panel discussion for my YouTube show called, *"New Year, Same God, No More Excuses."* That topic was based on Luke 14:15-24. A master prepared a huge supper and was ready for his guests to come over to eat. So, he sent his servant to go get those who were invited. However, one by one they each made an excuse (verses 18, 19, and 20):

1. *I have bought a piece of ground, and I must go and see it.* He was saying, "My job is more important than going to the supper."

2. *I have bought five yoke of oxen, and I am going to test them.* He was saying, "My possessions are more important than going to the supper.

3. *I have married a wife, and therefore I cannot come.* He was saying, "My relationship is more important than going to the supper."

The master was angry and told the servant,

"Go out quickly into the streets and lanes of the city, and bring in here the poor and the maimed and the lame and the blind." There were still room and the master told the servant, "Go out into the highways and hedges, and compel them to come in, that my house may be filled."

The master said that those men who were invited but made an excuse would not taste his supper. This parable Jesus taught is an illustration of His return (the Rapture). Jesus has gone to prepare a place for us. He's preparing something great for us and He will come back and take every believer back with Him. The invitation has been extended to all people but it's up to each person to accept that invitation.

"For God so loved the world, that He gave His only begotten Son, that whosoever believeth in Him should not perish, but have everlasting life." John 3:16 (KJV)

God has given this world a precious gift, His Son, Jesus Christ. As much as the Gospel is going out all over the world, there are still so many who are lost. When I see those who are lost, it bothers me. Something that really leave me lost for words are those who know about Jesus and know he's real but flat out choose to live the way they want to live and make excuses when it comes to making time for the Lord.

I would be lying to myself and to you if I didn't tell you this next part. This is something I am trying to get over. It makes me angry when some admit they need the Lord and have the opportunity to start developing a relationship with Him but then choose to go in the opposite direction. I understand that change is not an event but a process; however, when are you going to start your process? Even some want to blame God for their situation. The reason it makes me angry is there are people who are truly hungry for the Lord but are still confused on how to fill the hunger. Why throw the Lord to the side and blame Him for what's going on in your life? The Lord is too good to be disrespected and treated like he's the enemy.

My dear friends, don't get so caught up in your earthly life that you miss out on life through Jesus Christ. Stop with the excuses and realize that this invitation is an invitation of a lifetime. We may not know when the Rapture will take place or when life will end on this side. We do know that we will leave this earth and will have to spend eternity somewhere. What Jesus can do for you is way more than what your job, possessions, and relationship can do for you. Yes, I agree, it's good to have a job, nice things, and a great relationship. But at the end of the day, what are those things really doing for you?

During the COVID-19 pandemic, so much time has been made available but there are so many that are not taking notice of how important this time is. So many people panicked when COVID-19 started spreading all over the World. They were afraid for their life. Imagine how the World will respond when the Rapture happens. Imagine how it will be. It will be an event that will happen across the World and for the believers in Christ it will be a joyous day because they will be with Jesus in the clouds. But for those left behind, it will not be a joyous day at all!

9
Jesus Is Waiting For You

I want to extend an invitation to you to accept Christ. I do not want to end this book without doing this. This is your time to give Jesus Christ your life.

I have talked about John 3:16 a lot in this book. In John 3:17, Jesus tells us that God did not send Jesus into the world to condemn the world. He was sent into the world that we might be saved through Him.

You may feel torn down by life and want to feel whole. Jesus is the answer. Welcome Him into your life right now my dear friend. I'm not going to put a sinner's prayer in this book. Say your own prayer to the Lord right now. Don't worry about those around you or worry about what people will say. Confess your sins, repent of your sins (ask God to give you strength to turn away from your sins) and declare Jesus Christ as your Lord and Savior.

"If you confess with your mouth the Lord Jesus and believe in your heart that God has raised Him from the dead, you will be saved."
Romans 10:9 NKJV

Don't worry about your past or how some people are going to bring up your past. Remember that God is a forgiving God! Through accepting

Jesus Christ, you are a new creation! The old is in the past and your life is now brand new.

"Therefore, if any man be in Christ, he is a new creature: old things are passed away; behold, all things are become new."
2 Corinthians 5:17 KJV

Today, when you hear His voice, harden not your heart. Let Jesus Christ come into your heart and save your soul! He's waiting for you to make your move. He has His arms opened wide for you. Claim this free gift in the name of the Father, in the name of the Son, and in the name of the Holy Spirit. Amen.

Do not turn this page if you have not accepted Jesus Christ as your Lord and Savior. Tomorrow is not promised. See Jesus for who He is right now. He's ready to show you much and to take you to a place in life you thought you would never go. Freedom is in Jesus!

Through Him you get an Assurance Policy. By accepting Him, when you leave this earth, Heaven will be your home. When we all get to Heaven, it will be a day of rejoicing just to see Jesus. What a glorious day of victory.

It's great to have a relationship with Jesus

now on Earth, but what an awesome thing to know that one day we will be face to face with Him! What a glorious day that will be!

10
One Last Thought

M y last thoughts...

- Be the best you can in life.

- Accomplish your goals and be all that you can.

- Only what you do for Christ will last!

- You will not profit anything if you succeed at so much in this world then lose your soul.

- Examine your life and make all the necessary changes.

- If Jesus is less in your life, make Him your life.

The Lord has answered your prayer by giving you more time and eliminating distractions.

Are you going to give Him your time and your attention?

Can you see Him now?

P.O. Box 453
Powder Springs, Georgia 30127
www.entegritypublishing.com
info@entegritypublishing.com
770.727.6517

www.ingramcontent.com/pod-product-compliance
Lightning Source LLC
Chambersburg PA
CBHW061919130726

47908CB00017B/2608